The
Rugby
Zombies

The Rugby Zombies

DAN ANTHONY

Pont

For
Bethan and Caitlin.

Published in 2010 by Pont Books, an imprint of
Gomer Press, Llandysul, Ceredigion, SA44 4JL

Reprinted 2011, 2012, 2013, 2014

ISBN 978 1 84851 167 5

A CIP record for this title is available from the British Library.

This book is published with the financial support of the
Welsh Books Council.

Printed and bound in Wales at
Gomer Press, Llandysul, Ceredigion

Prologue

Arwel didn't get picked.

After the final practice session, the games teacher chose someone else. To be fair to Mr Edwards, Arwel did not cover himself in glory. It was ages before he got the ball . . . and then he dropped it.

But Arwel knew he could do better. At home he went over the session and worked out what he should have done . . . *A little sidestep, a chip ahead, the ball bounces back into his hands, still three to beat, but he smashes past them and scores a try under the posts!*

Chapter 1

Arwel lived in a small rugby-mad town in south Wales. On the walls of his school were photographs of all the Old Boys who had played for Wales. Some of the photos were so old that the faded colours made them look like the ghosts of the men they had become. The school wasn't special. It had long corridors, classrooms with big windows and a flat roof which someone fell through at least once a term. They were always trying to fix the building, which had been put up hastily in the early 1980s. The governors had agreed to build a new science block to honour a former pupil who had become a famous scientist and given the school a lot of money. It would soon have a new name: the Malcolm Jenkins High School, *Ysgol Gyfun Malcolm Jenkins*.

The pupils preferred their own name for it: Aberscary Comprehensive.

*

Arwel's mother was very hard-working. His father was interested in finding out about new spiritual experiences. The funny thing about his parents, thought Arwel, was that neither of them ever stuck at anything very long. His mother was always trying for new jobs and his dad was always trying out different religions. He'd sampled most of the main ones but, for lots of reasons, they didn't work for him. At the moment he was giving Buddhism a go.

The one religion which didn't change for Arwel's dad, though, was rugby. He loved it. In Aberscary he was known as 'Mr Rugby'.

Arwel's mum worked for a firm of solicitors. Before that she worked in a hotel. Before that she was a nurse. She helped out regularly in The Rose and Crown, her brother's pub up the road.

Arwel had an older sister, Tania. She was in Year 12 and had a boyfriend, Steve; he was in year 13, drove a Fiesta and played rugby for the school and the district. On international days Steve had a job at the Millennium Stadium. He wore a yellow jacket with 'marshal' on the back, and a special armband. Once or twice Tania had taken Arwel to watch him play. The first time, Steve got concussed and had to leave the field. He said that the world really was spinning and he could see psychedelic cows. The other time he scored a try.

On the mantelpiece at home there were photos: loads of Tania winning medals for swimming, netball, even cheerleading, but there was just one of Arwel. It was a team photo for the local under-sevens and he was wearing a green rugby jersey. He looked really stupid, with combed-down brown hair. There were photos of his dad from years back when he played rugby for Aberscary; there were some new ones of

his dad in his Aberscary committee blazer. The
were pictures of his parents' wedding, his grans a
granddads, his cousins having birthdays, getting
married, holding babies. Arwel knew it would be
great to have another picture of himself up there,
playing for the school, but, try as he might, he just
couldn't get into the team and, consequently, onto
the mantelpiece. He didn't really like the photographs
because they reminded him of what he hadn't done.

Arwel didn't have a huge number of friends and
only really bothered with a couple of people: Glen
Sarapoglu and Martin Trezise. In the evenings he'd
meet them outside the Spar shop and they'd chill,
especially in the winter. They liked seeing who was
out and about on the street and what was going
on. On one thing they were all agreed: there wasn't
anything exciting to do in their town.

Glen was a bit of liability; he was always in trouble.
He was tall, with big wild dark eyes and mad curly
hair that stuck up all over the place. Miss Tavernspite,
the head of lower school, said he was bad news but
Arwel knew he wasn't really. He was a good laugh.
He played rugby sometimes; quite often he'd get sent
off. Glen used to say that if the opposing players were
going to dish it out then it was OK to do it back to
them. If you can't take it, you shouldn't dish it out.

Martin didn't play rugby at all. He said he preferred
surfing, not that he had a surfboard, not that they
lived by the sea. He said games were a waste of time.

Martin always looked hungry, like he hadn't eaten for days. In the school show at Christmas they made him play Oliver because he looked so malnourished. He had blue eyes and weedy hair which meant that all the mums went 'Aah' when he said, 'Please, sir, can I have some more?' In fact Martin wasn't malnourished at all; his mum said that feeding him was like shovelling crisps into a black hole.

Apart from spending quite a lot of their spare time outside the Spar, they often stayed up at Martin's because his house was at the edge of town. Behind it were the mountain and the forest. When they were small they'd made a den there. Now it was just somewhere to go to get out of the way.

On Wednesday night they'd been to the Spar shop, chilling, and then, because Glen had been messing with the wheelie bins, they'd had to make a quick getaway. So they went up to the forest behind Martin's place. By the time they'd arrived it was dark. It was strange up there, like no-man's land. If you looked one way you could see the whole valley lit up below, with houses, streetlights, shops, and cars creeping around the roads like tiny spaceships in the November mist. And if you turned around and looked up the other way, all you could see was the grey outline of the mountain curved like an animal's back, and the forest, a black place, a hole in the night with nothing in it. Martin used to say that it was the edge of the civilised universe: look down and you see Aberscary and all its

10

boring brightness; look up and you don't really know what you're looking at. Arwel always thought that Martin's back-garden wall was the border between the known and the unknown universe. That was cool.

Arwel, Glen and Martin sat on the wall and looked down on Aberscary. The street lights made it look exciting, which they all knew it wasn't. The only way to liven it up was to do something. Sometimes they'd play a game called 'crisis'. You had to look down the valley and find something, say a lorry, driving down the A470 to Cardiff. Then you'd have to say what the crisis was.

'In the back of the blue tanker there's radioactive material from that factory over there.' Arwel pointed across the valley at the industrial estate. 'That's where they make nuclear weaponry; it's a Mafia tanker and they're going to hold the Government to ransom.'

Glen and Martin weren't really listening. 'Let's have a war,' said Glen.

'Let's not,' said Arwel. 'We'll get beaten up.'

The last time they had a war it had been with the kids from the school in the next town, Aberlairy. It had started because the Aberscary Comprehensive kids beat up an Aberlairy boy called Ieuan Stainer. He'd been messing about outside the Aberscary Spar although it was generally agreed that Aberlairy actually had a bigger and better Spar of its own. As retaliation for his beating, Ieuan Stainer and his gang had put a brick through the Aberscary Spar window.

There was only one possible outcome: Aberscary Comprehensive declared war and after school a large crowd set out for Aberlairy, but by the time they arrived, only ten of them were left. Three of the ten were Arwel, Glen and Martin.

Martin looked across the valley. 'We should nick something,' he said thoughtfully.

'Like what?' asked Glen.

'I dunno,' said Martin. 'We could hide it up here.'

'What?' asked Arwel.

'The thing we steal,' said Martin.

Glen's big brown eyes lit up: he had it – an idea. 'The wheelie bins,' he said. 'Let's nick the wheelie bins from the Spar.'

Arwel and Martin looked at Glen; it wasn't a bad idea.

'They'd never expect anybody to nick their bins,' said Glen. 'Imagine the look on their faces when they find them not there!'

'We can hide them up here,' said Martin. 'Nobody'd think to look here and there are no security cameras.'

'Brilliant,' said Glen, 'it's brilliant.'

Arwel wasn't convinced. He couldn't quite see what the point was. But he couldn't quite see why they shouldn't do it either – apart from the obvious reasons. Nobody had ever taken anything as big and strange as the Spar's wheelie bins. That was cool. And the people in the shop treated the kids really badly. Only two at a time were allowed in, because the owners reckoned they stole stuff. But the kids only took stuff because the Spar people were nasty to them. 'Borrowing' the bins would teach them a lesson especially if they returned them later. On the other hand, thought Arwel, it wasn't going to be easy. But then again, that's what made it a cool idea.

Just then the wind picked up. It was cold, really cold, so cold it blew through the three of them. It made them shiver in their bones. It happened like that sometimes up on the mountain. They looked at each other, then back towards the forest. It was completely black inside. The pine trees rustled like a dog shivering. The wind came from in there. A lot of people found the forest spooky and said it was haunted. But Arwel knew it wasn't. He had been going up there for ages. It was just a cold wind that made you feel spooked. That was what was cool about the forest; it was a chilled-out zone.

Martin said there were lots of other reasons why it seemed spooky: people kept chickens and other animals which made funny noises. There were horses on the mountain too: they got lost sometimes; there were even tramps who slept in the woods from time to time; you could hear them talking.

In the end the boys went home: it was too cold to stay hanging about. But at least they knew what to do next. They would 'borrow' the wheelie bins from the Spar shop.

Chapter 2

The next day, Arwel arrived home from school to find two unusual things. His mum was home. And so was his sister. When Arwel entered the kitchen they stopped talking, like he was interrupting something. So he just went to the fridge and pretended he hadn't noticed.

'What do you want, Arwel?' asked Tania, who had, he thought, been crying.

'Cheese!' said Arwel flatly.

'Don't be like that,' said his mum, unzipping her laptop bag.

'Like what?' asked Arwel, fiddling with the packet. 'There's no law against eating cheese.' He looked at Tania: her face was red; she'd definitely been crying; her make-up was all streaky and her blond straight hair was sticky-uppy.

His mum explained: 'Tania's been having a bit of trouble with Steve.'

Tania was always having trouble with Steve; all she ever talked about with her friends was Steve. And they were just the same: boyfriend trouble was their sole topic of conversation. As far as Arwel could see, they needed their problems. Without them they had nothing to talk about.

'I like Steve,' he said, slicing the cheese into thin strips.

'I've dumped him, if you must know,' said Tania, sighing. 'We're just not right together.'

'Oh dear,' said Arwel's mum, plugging in her laptop.

Arwel poured himself an orange juice and picked up the cheese. 'You'll get back together; he can't have done anything that bad,' he said, heading off for the living room.

'He's only got himself injured,' wailed Tania. 'We're supposed to be going to Giovanni's and Steve has gone and hospitalised himself.'

'What happened?' asked Arwel, suddenly interested. 'Who was he playing?'

'I'm sick of rugby,' moaned Tania. 'There's no doubt that in this relationship I come second. He never puts me first.'

Arwel had heard this before; so had his mum. Tania always wanted Steve to put her first. If she wasn't first then she wasn't happy. Arwel didn't understand her. Nobody put him first and he didn't mind. He wanted to be first. But he just wasn't. He couldn't even get into the school team. Steve played at district level. You had to respect that, thought Arwel.

'Is he still in hospital?' he asked.

'Discharged,' muttered Tania.

'You should go and see him,' said Mum.

'I texted him; I said it was over with me and him,' said Tania. 'He's so selfish with his injuries.'

Arwel's mum sighed and sat down in front of the

laptop. Tania took out her phone and started texting people like mad. Arwel went into the living room and turned on his computer.

Glen was messaging Arwel the real news. Steve had got injured, but he was playing in a trial. Even though he'd had to leave the pitch, they'd picked him. Wales Under 19s. Arwel went back into the kitchen. Tania wasn't crying any more. She was eating digestive biscuits and drinking tea.

'You'll never guess what?' said Arwel.

Mum and Tania looked at him. 'What?' they said.

'Steve is going to play for Wales.'

Mum looked at Tania. Tania looked at Arwel. 'Really?' she said.

'Didn't you know?' asked Mum.

'I didn't ask. I must have dumped him before he could tell me.' A look of mild panic flickered across Tania's face. She bit her knuckles. She knew, in black and white terms, that she'd made a mistake. 'I've got to go out,' she said.

And she went. But she was back almost at once. 'Arwel, you're coming with me.'

Before he could wolf any more cheese Arwel was on his way.

*

Tania, with Arwel in tow, walked up to Steve's place which was on a new estate called 'The Granthams' just behind the supermarket. Steve's house had a front garden and a garage. Tania didn't want to be seen so they hung about behind one of the trees in a neighbour's garden whilst she briefed Arwel. She told him to go and see Steve and talk about rugby. He was to tell Steve that she was really sorry about his injuries and that she didn't want to dump him really. No way was Steve to know that she was outside, hiding behind the tree.

Arwel thought this was just plain stupid but he liked Steve and he wanted to find out whether he really was going to play for Wales. That was so cool. So Arwel did as he was told. He walked down the drive to the front door and gave the bell a good press.

Steve's mum answered the door. She was a tall woman with brown eyes and bright red lips. She looked at Arwel. 'You've heard,' she said, pointing to Arwel's shoes.

Arwel took his shoes off, remembering Steve's mum's thick white carpets. When his shoes were off she let him in. Her carpets were, he thought, the opposite of her hair, which was short and black.

'He's in the living room, no more concussed than usual, I reckon,' she said. 'Tell him I'll bring him some more tea. Would you like some? Biscuit?'

Arwel said he would: he liked Steve's place; the carpets were really warm on his toes.

Steve was lying on the sofa, watching TV. Arwel was careful to find out as much as he could about the trial, the game and the Welsh cap before he told

Steve about Tania. As soon as he did, Steve was busy texting. Thirty seconds later, Tania was at the front door.

In the end they offered Arwel a lift home in the Fiesta just to get rid of him. On the way, Steve drove past the Spar. Arwel looked hard for the wheelie bins. They weren't there. That was awesome. Glen and Martin must have been busy already.

When Steve dropped him off, Arwel waited until the car disappeared round the corner. Then he walked up to the woods behind Martin's house.

It was getting dark and that cold wind was blowing again. Arwel looked around for Martin and Glen but he couldn't see them. It didn't matter because he knew exactly where they'd be – in their old den in amongst the pine trees. It was an easy walk because the forest was thick and nothing much grew there, apart from pine trees. The ground was soft, covered with old pine needles and twigs, and his feet sunk into the spongy, springy mat of needles every time he took a step.

Arwel knew his way around in the forest, and quickly found the old den. There, as he expected, stood two great big wheelie bins. He could only just make them out. In the gloom of the forest, in the fading light, they looked alien. He shouted for Glen and Martin, but heard nothing apart from the crack of trees in the strange, puffy, pine-fresh wind.

Then Arwel felt something. A cold breeze coming

from deep in the woods. It was so cold; it just blew straight into him and seemed to freeze him inside. He didn't know why but suddenly he felt very scared, almost as if he was being watched. He stared around him, straining his eyes, but the daylight had gone. He could make out the shapes of the tree trunks. He thought he could see things moving between them. Perhaps it was just the branches making shadows in the night. And then there was the sound, the long, low ghostly moans. He didn't like it at all.

Arwel shouted for Martin and Glen again. But the wind just got stronger and colder and the moans got louder, so loud he couldn't ignore them. Without stopping to think, Arwel ran. He ran as fast as he could, skidding on the pine needles, trying to sidestep the trees, following the path out of the wood. He made it, but he didn't look back; he kept running down one road, down the next, into the orange glow of the street lights. After a while he stopped and glanced over his shoulder. There was nothing behind him. Nobody was following him.

He walked home, telling himself off for being dumb.

Chapter 3

The next day Arwel, Martin and Glen stood looking at the updated team sheet on the board outside the changing rooms. Arwel thought Martin and Glen had been behaving strangely all morning; they kept whispering to one another and smirking at him. Now he thought he'd found out why.

'Year 9 Rugby – First XV,' said the list. The usual names were up there, including Glen, number 2, hooker. But at number 11, there was a new name – Arwel Williams. At last he'd been selected to play for the Firsts. This had never happened before. He'd played for the Seconds, he'd been a sub for the Firsts, but had never had a game. Now he'd made it.

He knew why. Gwyndaf, 'the Flying Fist' as he liked to be known, had gone to Llangrannog on a Welsh course; Faisal, the second-fastest boy in the year, was sick, and Ceri Jones, the utility back, had been suspended from school for swearing at a teacher. Mr Edwards had just run out of players.

Glen gave Arwel a congratulatory punch in the arm. 'Man, you've made it,' he laughed.

Arwel recoiled, rubbing his arm – it really hurt – Glen didn't know his own strength. 'Only because of crime, disease and Welsh,' said Arwel. 'I'm the last option.'

'In sport you have to take the breaks: it doesn't matter how you get a chance; when you get one you grab it,' said Martin, 'or you walk away, like me. You wouldn't catch me going out there to get soaking wet, freezing cold and beaten up by a bunch of dur-brains from Ponty!'

Glen laughed. 'Don't worry, we'll sort them first; it'll be a doddle – they're scared of us. We've got . . . me,' he said, shaping to punch Arwel's arm again.

Arwel grabbed his fist and pushed it down. 'I know,' he said, 'that's good.' His mind was already racing ahead. Now, all he could think about was the game. His dad would be there. He hoped that he didn't mess it up. It would be terrible if he missed a tackle. He had to get it right. Dad would be on at him to come up the club again. He didn't know if he was ready to do that. Up the club they were really serious. On the other hand, if he played well, he might get onto the mantelpiece.

'But you're going to have to sort yourself out,' said Martin, 'mentally speaking.'

Glen looked straight into Arwel's eyes. Then he made a long, low moaning noise, exactly like the sound Arwel had heard in the forest. Then Glen and Martin started laughing uncontrollably. Arwel didn't understand. What was the matter with them?

Martin explained about the wheelie bins. They'd taken them to the den. Arwel said he knew. He said he'd seen them. Then Martin started to laugh again, really hard. By the time they'd got the bins to the den, it was dark, he said. They'd heard something; somebody was behind them, following them. They figured it was someone from the Spar; so they hid in the bins. They were well scared. When they heard Arwel shouting they were so relieved. The zombie noises were a joke. 'Wicked!' said Martin. 'Your reaction . . .'

Arwel looked at the pair of them giggling.

'We're sorry, man,' said Martin. 'But you really did make us laugh.'

'It was scary in there; don't forget I was on my own. There's something funny about that forest; I reckon it's haunted,' said Arwel.

'Yeah, by me and Martin,' said Glen. 'You have so got to sort out your head. *Sort out your brain before you play the game.*'

Arwel shrugged and smiled weakly. He didn't like being tricked. He didn't like the thought of Glen and Martin sniggering away at the bottom of the wheelie bins. But he could see it was the obvious thing to do: anyone would have done the same. The most important thing was that they had achieved their objective. They had nicked the wheelie bins. Not many people could say that.

Arwel's main problem, his only problem, was the game. He asked Glen to come over to the park that evening to practise kicking.

Chapter 4

Arwel arrived home from school to find his dad in the kitchen, talking on his mobile about a Buddhist retreat weekend in the countryside. Arwel went to fetch some cheese from the fridge before collecting his rugby ball. Dad finished the conversation quickly, throwing his phone down and punching Arwel on the arm in exactly the same place that Glen got him earlier.

'Gerroff, Dad,' Arwel shouted, rubbing his sore arm.

'Got to be tougher than that, boy, got to be a lot tougher than that – Mr Selected!' Dad started shadow-boxing around the kitchen.

'Dad, I'm sure fist-fighting doesn't count as a Buddhist technique,' complained Arwel.

His dad boxed his way in front of him and gave him a succession of rapid rabbit punches in the chest. 'Boxing would only be forbidden if it was violent,' he said, 'and this isn't violent – it's karmic.'

Arwel sighed; he noticed his father was wearing trainers and an old tracksuit.

'Come on, boy, we're going out,' said Dad.

'Where? Why?' asked Arwel.

'Training,' said Dad.

'Hold on a minute,' said Arwel. 'Who told you I got selected?'

'Hoof from the club,' said Dad.

Arwel looked down at the floor; this was bad. Things were already getting out of control. He began to wonder if this was going to be a rugby nightmare, not a dream. Hoof was the club's oldest player – he was also Wayne Hoof's dad. Wayne was the best outside half in Arwel's year. They were already talking about Wayne in Cardiff. He must have texted his dad that Arwel was in the team.

'Brilliant, boy, you come up the club this weekend; you should have a run around with the Thirds.'

Arwel nodded. He knew that all this interest from his dad depended on him playing well on Thursday. If he played badly he wouldn't want to go up the club for a run around with the Thirds. He'd prefer to go 'borrowing' wheelie bins.

The thing about his dad, thought Arwel, was that though he changed his other religions relatively frequently, rugby was a constant. So if you were getting cheesed off with, say, kosher chicken or fasting in Ramadan, you knew that it wouldn't last forever; the fast would be broken by something new. The only thing that never changed was rugby. His dad was the treasurer of the local club; he'd played for them when he was young; he'd been captain when he grew up; he'd painted the lines on the pitch; he'd walked to London to raise money for the clubhouse; he'd fought legal battles against developers to protect the sacred turf; he enjoyed a pint at the clubhouse every weekend (no matter what his religion was) and he went to meetings there almost every night. He was Mr Rugby in Aberscary and Mr Rugby was going to big this game up.

He'd be down on the school touchline with his two buddies, Benbow and Hoof, supporting Arwel like (he tried to think what they'd be like) 'crazed, wild, rabid bears'. Arwel said the words out loud. It wasn't a good prospect. His dad would probably get the local radio down there, and the newspaper.

He tried to persuade him not to come training, but Dad insisted. So the two of them went over the rec. to kick the ball about with Glen. In the end it was a laugh. His dad showed them how to do screw kicks; they did conversions and they almost lost the ball in the river.

After that, Dad went home to meditate; Arwel and Glen decided to call in at the Spar before going up to the forest to check on the wheelie bins. Outside the shop there was a notice. The police had been informed about the missing bins.

Up in the forest with Glen, Arwel had that same feeling. It was about the same time, six o'clock, dusk had fallen and night was grabbing at the world. Arwel was clearer about it now. It felt cold and he was sure they were being watched. They stood, silent, in the damp dark forest, looking at the eerie tubular shapes of the bins.

'Can you feel it?' asked Arwel.

'What?' asked Glen.

'That wind – it's not normal. It doesn't come from anywhere,' said Arwel.

Glen stood still, trying to feel the wind. The trees creaked. 'It's definitely spooky,' he said, 'but no more than it always was. It's just an ordinary spooky forest. There's hundreds of them around here.'

Then Arwel saw it – a figure; no more than ten metres away a person slid into the gloom. Arwel grabbed Glen. 'Look!' he hissed. 'There he goes. Come on.'

They ran after the shape – deeper into the forest. 'It's gonna be Martin, isn't it?' puffed Glen. 'He lives up here. He's freaking us out!'

'Oi, Martin!' yelled Arwel. 'Stop messing with our minds.'

They crashed deeper into the woods. But they lost the shape. It was like following a tracker, someone who knew the paths like his own backyard – someone like Martin.

Arwel held out his hand. They stopped running and stood still. Their breath was hot in the cold night air. It puffed out of their mouths like steam. They looked around them. Trees merged into one great black wooden wall.

Arwel shivered. 'OK, Martin, come on out, mun. This isn't a joke.' He couldn't see much. He strained his eyes, trying to make out shapes in the gloom. But it was so dark in there. Somewhere above them there was a sliver of a moon and hardly any stars. Then he saw it. Clear as day. For about half a second. One word came to Arwel; he shouted it as loud as he could: 'RUN!'

He grabbed Glen and shoved him back the way they came. They ran as fast as they could. Glen kept asking 'What's up?' but Arwel couldn't speak; he was too scared. He just ran. What he'd seen was real. What he'd seen was scary, really scary. Aberscary scary.

They ran out of the forest, down the side of the hill into Martin's street and hammered on his door. Martin's sister, Julie, answered it and let them in.

'Where's Martin?' demanded Arwel.

'In his room,' answered Julie.

They pushed her out of the way and barged into Martin's room. He was watching *EastEnders*.

'Hiya, boys,' he said, popping a prawn-cocktail crisp into his mouth.

Glen grabbed Martin and hauled him up. He shook him with his fists. 'Have you been messing with our minds?'

Martin asked what was going on.

Glen sat down and thought for a minute. He didn't actually know what Arwel had seen: 'I dunno,' he said. 'I just know it's spooky. Arwel saw something . . . terrible.'

'Look,' said Martin calmly, 'whatever Arwel saw in that forest was probably just a figment of his imagination; it's because we spooked him the other day.'

Glen nodded slowly. He looked pale and jumpy; his brown eyes were wide and he was breathing heavily. He kept walking to the window, pushing back the curtains and looking to see if they had been followed. 'I dunno,' he said. 'It was pretty scary in there. Arwel definitely saw something. I'm just not sure what it was.'

'Probably a cat,' said Martin, 'or a fox.'

Arwel shook his head. He knew exactly what he had seen. He looked at Glen; he looked at Martin, then he said it. 'I saw . . . a zombie.'

Chapter 5

At home the game was all Arwel's dad could think about. He was swept away on a wave of enthusiasm for his son's career. Perhaps this was the turning point – one day Arwel would put on the black-and-red jersey that he once wore, and play for Aberscary. On Wednesday evening he took Arwel into his meditation room, the spare bedroom, where he kept, amongst other things, his meditation drums. It was actually an ordinary drum kit which he'd borrowed from a bloke called Ned up at the rugby club. Ned was in a rock band called 'Ned Zeppelin', a tribute band which had started making money so he'd bought a bigger kit.

The room was painted light brown. It had a soft brown carpet; there were big purple floor-cushions from IKEA; there were little bells and candles and a small brass Buddha sitting cross-legged by the bass drum. Arwel sat on one of the cushions whilst his dad squeezed in behind his drum kit, tapping the bass pedal with his big foot as he pushed back the black curly hair at the side of his head. As he drummed he shouted to Arwel to imagine all sorts of good things happening on the rugby field. Arwel tried. He thought about slipping past the other players, booting the ball miles down the pitch, sliding over the line for a try. Dad did the same and for about ten minutes they sat there, entranced by the repetitive beat, thinking about playing fantastic rugby.

'I'm in the Millennium Stadium,' fantasised Dad, his black eyes flashing like olives on a pizza. 'I'm on a podium holding a huge trophy in my hand – you're there, boy, in your kit, there's a whole team of you. The crowd is going mad. They're singing. I'm the coach of the best team in history. We've won something big!'

Arwel enjoyed this game. It was much easier than the real thing. His dad kept tapping the drum with his big toe.

'OK, I'm on the wing, I've got the ball – we're in New Zealand. I'm skipping through huge tackles like I'm on a surfboard.'

Dad laughed: 'Brilliant, mun,' he shouted. 'I'm with you.'

After about half an hour he said that was enough: now all they had to do was take the positivity of the experience and transfer it into real life. Arwel thought that part of the exercise was probably going to be the most difficult, because, although he'd seen a lot of good pictures in his mind, there was one image which kept coming back. One bad picture he couldn't blot out. It was of him and Glen running for their lives in the forest. He knew it shouldn't be but when he asked himself which was more real: beating the All Blacks or being chased by a zombie, he always came up with the same answer – the zombie.

Chapter 6

It was Thursday morning, breakfast. Arwel was eating toast and marmalade. His dad was making more toast. His sister was straightening her blond hair and his mum was looking for the lead for her laptop. Arwel looked tired.

'You look exhausted,' said Mum.

'That's cos I am,' said Arwel.

'What's the matter, boy, you not sleeping properly?' said Dad. 'You gotta sleep, boy. Everybody sleeps before a game.'

'He's probably nervous,' said Tania smugly, glancing across at Arwel with a look which suggested that he had every right to be uncomfortable because he was rubbish at rugby.

'I doubt that very much,' said Dad. 'What did I teach you last night, Arwel?'

'Relaxation techniques, using the drum of peace,' said Arwel.

'Nice one,' said Dad.

'Oh dear,' said Mum, 'don't listen to all this, Arwel; he'll be Rastafarian next week.'

'Actually,' said Dad. 'I have already made good friends with the disciples of Haile Selassie. Jah is with you too, my boy.'

Arwel's mum looked at his dad as if she thought

he was nuts. She put her arm around Arwel. 'Don't worry about the game,' she said. 'You do look tired.'

'He's scared,' said Tania.

Arwel wriggled out of his mother's grip, picked up his kit in the hall and ran off for school. He couldn't tell them the truth. He was worried about the game, of course; he didn't want to mess up. But there was something much scarier on his mind. He couldn't sleep because of the zombie. He'd been lying in bed all night, thinking about the shape in the forest. He'd seen its face; maybe it wasn't even a face, just white with holes for eyes.

Arwel had also been thinking about Glen. Glen hadn't seen the shape, but he'd felt something and in the end even Martin had agreed that it was theoretically possible for there to be a zombie in the wood behind his house, although he felt that it was strange that he had never noticed it in the past. As he hurried to school Arwel tried to make himself think about rugby. He tried to remember his dad's drumming and the dreams about scoring tries. But the nightmare in the woods kept coming back, again and again. His thoughts went round and round. His dad had kept on about being focussed, being calm. He knew he was neither of these things. He didn't know what to concentrate on: the rugby or the zombie.

The day in school passed slowly. At break and dinner time he'd seen Glen and Martin and they'd talked about the zombie. Martin wanted to use the wheelie bins to make a zombie trap. Glen wasn't so sure about this; he said that although he hadn't actually seen anything, he felt that they shouldn't mess around with forces beyond their control. Martin laughed – he wanted proof. Glen reluctantly agreed.

At one-thirty Arwel had to go to the changing rooms and join the team. All the boys from his year were there. They were noisy and enthusiastic. Arwel, on the other hand, couldn't concentrate.

Jack Wilson, the captain, came over to him. 'Hiya, Arwel; you'll be fine. Anybody gives you any trouble, let me and the boys know and we'll sort them out.'

'Ta,' said Arwel, as he pulled on his Aberscary Comprehensive School rugby jersey – red-and-black, the same as the club team.

He tied on his shiny new boots and clattered out of the changing room with the other boys, their studs pinging on the concrete before squelching into the muddy grass.

Mr Edwards, the games teacher, appeared, wearing his tracksuit and a little green bobble hat. He blew his whistle and the boys gathered around him in a big circle. 'Good, boys, excellent, well done,' he enthused, clenching his fist.

Arwel looked around; they hadn't done anything yet and Mr Edwards was already praising them. 'Enthusiasm, boys, enthusiasm, one-hundred-and-ten-per-cent commitment – that's what this is about.'

He caught Arwel's eye. 'Good to see you here, Arwel; you're on the wing. Show them the space outside, then hit them there; you'll do well,' he said. 'Your dad was great at doing that; he never missed a tackle.'

Arwel tried to look enthusiastic as Mr Edwards talked about the strengths and weaknesses of the Ponty team.

Glen looked around, slightly bored, because Mr Edwards always said the same thing. Glen knew what was coming next. The games teacher took a great breath of air and looked up into the grey sky as if searching for inspiration. When it came, he spoke again. 'This is a game: there are two teams; you can win it,' he bellowed. 'Give me twenty.'

All the boys threw themselves on the floor and started doing press-ups, grumbling at the same time.

'Come on, come on!' shouted Mr Edwards.

As Arwel did his press-ups he remembered the drumming. For the first time in two days he forgot about the zombie. He was going to play for the school; he had been selected; this was real rugby. He thought about how he would come bursting through the line, flip the ball to Glen, loop inside him, take a pass and score under the posts. That was going to be a cool moment.

The pitch was a little way away from the main school building, between the netball courts and the nature reserve. When they arrived, the Ponty players were already jogging around the touchline. On the halfway line there was a small crowd, a few parents, a couple of mates; his dad was there, so were Steve and Tania and his dad's mate Benbow, hidden deep inside his anorak; next to him stood Hoof, Wayne's dad, and half of the netball team, who had just won their game against the same school.

Glen trotted over to Arwel and punched him in the arm. 'Under the posts, Arwel. I've got a good feeling about this,' he said.

'Yeah,' said Arwel.

It was a home game so Mr Edwards was reffing. The home team lost the toss, and took up their positions on the field. On the left wing, Arwel found himself standing close to Dad, Tania, Steve and the netballers.

'Go on, Arwel,' yelled his dad.

Arwel looked at the netball girls: their legs were pink and cold; one of them, a girl called Beth Fenwick, shouted, 'Come on, Arwel!' He was surprised. He didn't think she even knew who he was.

Steve looked cool; Tania held his arm, looking bored; Dad looked cold in his tracksuit bottoms and his red-and-black Aberscary jersey.

They kicked off. The ball went to the forwards and things started. By half-time it was clear it wasn't going to be a high-scoring game. Arwel had the ball twice, but he couldn't make a break. He didn't drop the ball though and he made a couple of good tackles. It was actually quite a good game. The fans were still keen and Steve had been shouting encouragement to the team, which made everyone feel good. Glen had only been warned for fighting twice and the rest of the boys in the pack were gradually wearing down their opponents.

At half-time they made a circle around Mr Edwards for the team talk. He was very enthusiastic: 'Good stuff, boys, excellent commitment, brilliant one-hundred-and-ten-per-cent stuff. But we're not getting through. I want to try a move. Arwel, you've got to come round off your wing, take the ball from Wayne, make an extra man, draw the tackle and put Gilligan, who'll be breaking into the line from fullback, in for a try.'

Arwel nodded. Gilligan looked at Arwel. He had clear blue eyes, short brown hair and a face like thunder. 'Do we have to use him?' he asked.

Arwel knew Gilligan didn't like him. He didn't much like Gilligan. Gilligan stared contemptuously at him with cold blue eyes.

Mr Edwards didn't appreciate being questioned by his students. 'Arwel's a new player, an unknown force. The Ponty boys are marking the rest of you off the pitch but they won't mark Arwel. He's a good player; he can put you away for a try. Now shut it, Gilligan, or I'll drop you. Does everybody understand the move?' he asked, screwing up his face with enthusiasm.

Arwel understood the move all right, but not when they were supposed to do it. But Mr Edwards was moving on. 'On your call, Wayne,' he said. Wayne Hoof was tough but taciturn; he nodded.

'What's the call?' asked Glen, wiping mud out of his hair.

'Bananas,' said Mr Edwards.

Mo, the lock forward, spoke. 'It can't be "bananas": that's what we use for the short line-out,' he said.

Mr Edwards thought for a moment. Mo was right – 'bananas' had been used up. He needed another word. 'Thinking on your feet, Mohammed, brilliant, you're absolutely one-hundred-and-ten-per-cent right. And clearly one-hundred-and-ten-per-cent committed. We can't say "bananas". Someone, quick, give us another call.'

'Sausages,' said Connor, the scrum half, nervously shifting from foot to foot; he was a small, thin boy with freckles and long wispy hair. He was also incredibly fast.

Glen spoke: 'Isn't "sausages" a bit hard to say?'

'No harder than "bananas"!' said Wayne.

'We need something short,' said skipper Jack Wilson; the call is "Arwel".'

'Won't they know that's me?' asked Arwel.

'They don't know you,' shouted Mr Edwards. 'This is your first game. They know everyone else. But they don't know you: the call is "Arwel". Brilliant thinking, Jack; they'll never expect that.'

Arwel nodded. He could see that this sounded reasonable – but he could also see a problem. If the

Ponty boys did know who he was, then it wasn't exactly the most secret code in the world. To him it seemed as if it might be the same as saying 'get Arwel'.

But Mr Edwards was convinced: 'One-hundred-and-twenty-five-per-cent imaginative thinking, Jack,' he enthused. 'Come on, boys. We've done the hard work; now let's get the points.'

The second half started and Arwel followed the game from the wing. He kept in position; he caught the kicks that came his way; he dropped back to support the fullback when he needed to; he came up to pressurise the Ponty boys when they had the ball. When he kicked he found touch, when he tackled he hit his opposite wing and when he got the ball he played safe and secure. He cut in, looked for support, kept the ball alive, made the hard yards. Arwel was enjoying himself. His dad wouldn't shut up, Steve was impressed, and Beth from the netball team was rooting for him. Arwel even smiled at her. The game was going like a dream. Somehow, that drumming stuff he did with Dad was working; it made him feel good about what he was doing and because he felt good, he did well. But the team couldn't score.

Then, about fifteen minutes from time, at a scrum just outside the Ponty twenty-two, Arwel heard the word and the word was 'Arwel'. The problem was he couldn't decide who had said it. Was it his dad or Steve on the touchline? Or his skipper, Jack Wilson?

Or somebody else on the pitch? He didn't know if the word was attached to others like 'come on' or whether it was the single word 'Arwel' which meant that the move had been called.

Arwel froze for a moment, watching the scrum. The two sets of forwards engaged in the fading light. Mr Edwards stood next to the scrum halves. The ball was just about to go into play. Since Arwel was on the wing he was too far away from anyone to ask whether the move had been called or not. He just knew that he'd heard his name. He felt confused. He tried to work it out; there wasn't much time. He figured that the game was nearly over; if they were going to make the move it had to be now. He could see that they were close enough to the Ponty try line. He hesitated as he weighed things up. Had the move been called or not? He had to make a decision: run to the centre of the field, take the ball from Wayne and pass to Gilligan or stay put and play safe. He couldn't ask anyone because that would completely remove the factor of surprise.

He looked behind him at Gilligan, but he just smiled as if he knew something was wrong. Arwel had to think on his own. As Connor dropped the ball into the scrum Arwel made his decision. He decided to risk it – probably, he thought, it was the call. The move was on. He ran, off his wing towards his own centres on the opposite side of the pitch.

But the ball came out on the Ponty side. The Ponty boys were tired, but they weren't stupid. Their scrum half had spotted Arwel sprinting off towards the other side of the pitch. He flipped the ball to his winger who practically walked down the touchline Arwel should have been blocking just as he was going as fast as he could in the wrong direction.

With Arwel miles out of position, his whole team and everybody on the touchline shouting at him, the Ponty boys scored. Too late, Arwel realised it had gone wrong. It was a disaster. It wasn't the move after all.

The Aberscary boys stood under the posts as Ponty lined up the conversion. Nobody said anything. Arwel muttered under his breath stuff about the stupid call; he knew that using 'Arwel' was dumb. He was right. That didn't help though. The fact was he had given away the winning try. Jack Wilson put his hand on his shoulder. 'Not your fault,' he said.

Arwel hung his head as Gilligan barged past him. 'Your fault,' he hissed.

The last ten minutes on the wing were terrible for Arwel. The supporters were silent, the netball girls drifted off, only his dad shouted encouragement – but it was useless.

The Ponty boys scored again. Glen got into a fight and Mr Edwards sent him off. In the end it was rubbish. Arwel knew he'd blown his chance; they'd never ask him to play again. They'd lost and it was his fault. They crawled back into the changing rooms, silent. Mr Edwards came to see them before they got into the showers. His round brown face was kind of knotted up.

'Well done, boys,' he said in his usual stupidly up-beat way. 'You gave one-hundred-and-ten-per-cent . . . but it wasn't enough.'

Gilligan said, 'We'd have won if it wasn't for that Arwel.'

And then it all kicked off. Gilligan yelled at Arwel. Arwel shouted that he knew the call was stupid; Glen thumped Gilligan; Jack Wilson smashed his head into his own locker in frustration. In the end someone had to grab Gilligan and hold him down to stop him from attacking Arwel.

When everybody calmed down Mr Edwards told the boys to get showered and go home. Nobody said any more.

It wasn't much better at home. Arwel's dad stayed upstairs, doing his Buddhist drumming. All Arwel could hear was this kind of repetitive thumping. His mum worked on her laptop and Tania and Steve went out. In the end, Arwel went out too. He didn't want to see Glen or Martin, so he didn't go to the Spar. He took the road around the rec. and followed it up towards the mountain. On the way a car passed him. It stopped and a window slid down. Arwel watched as a head appeared in the window; it was Beth from the netball team – her dad was driving her somewhere.

'Hey, Arwel, don't worry about today. I thought

you played really well; it wasn't your fault,' she smiled. 'I saw what happened.'

Arwel couldn't help smiling back. 'Thanks,' he said. 'It was my fault though; I should have got them to stick to "bananas".'

The window slid back up and Beth's car purred off down the road.

*

Without thinking, Arwel arrived at the forest. Without thinking, he walked straight in; without thinking, he walked deep into the trees. He passed the wheelie bins; he pushed further into the woods and sat on the floor at the spot where he saw the zombie, or where he thought he saw the zombie.

'What a loser,' he thought. Years of rugby effort and his career had ended because he misheard a stupid call. There would be no going back. Rugby for him was over. A spectator only, he would never play for the district. He would never play for his region. He would never play for Wales. He would never get another picture onto the mantelpiece.

Slowly it grew darker and colder. This time Arwel wasn't scared. Nothing could be worse than that misheard call. If there were zombies in the forest he wanted to meet them. He wanted the zombies to come and get him. He wanted to fight them. That would show everybody. He'd kill the zombies and they'd kill him. A twig cracked nearby and a figure stepped out of the gloom.

Nothing can quite prepare you for the shock of seeing a zombie. Suddenly Arwel lost all the feeling in his body. It was like being frozen alive. His face turned to putty, his hands went rigid and he began to shake. The thing standing in front of him was half-dead.

The creature's legs were purple, with bones sticking out through the skin, and mushrooms growing on the collar of his faded red rugby shirt. His neck was a mixture of sinew and spine and his eyes balanced in their sockets like snooker-balls overhanging their pockets. His hair grew in splodges over the one remaining ear. He had long grey fingernails and bony feet pointing out through a pair of ancient rugby boots. There was a strange smell, too, like a combination of fungus and chip fat.

Arwel tried to stand up, to defend himself: he didn't want to die after all. He had a lot to live for. OK, so he misheard the move: worse things happen. But he couldn't shift. His legs were frozen with fear. And that cold wind was blowing through him again. It felt like his flesh was being ripped from his bones.

Arwel stared at the zombie, vaguely registering the three Prince of Wales feathers on the mouldering red rag hanging from his skeletal chest. 'Oh no,' whispered Arwel, 'a rugby zombie.' The worst kind imaginable. Caught forever on the bridge between injury time and the final whistle, rugby zombies had to be bad news.

'Why did you come back?' asked the zombie. 'You knew I was here.'

Arwel didn't really know the answer. 'I wanted to see you,' he said.

The zombie came closer. 'Nobody has ever wanted to see me,' he said. Then he straightened up and gestured with his arm. Bits fell off it. 'Nobody has ever wanted to see . . . us,' he added.

Arwel looked around. It just got worse. From all sides rugby zombies appeared, dragging their misshapen, decomposing bodies through the pine trees until he was surrounded. They all wore the same kit, ancient Welsh jerseys rotting on their bodies, the numbers on their backs peeling off like scabs from skin. The zombies were bathed in silvery light, a white glow which seemed to emanate from them: bright, but cold, like snow.

'You are the first person ever to find us and come back for a second look,' observed the zombie Arwel took to be the leader.

The others looked at him. Arwel noticed that they didn't seem very threatening. In their eyes, what was left of them, he didn't see hate or anger: they looked more like dogs, frightened dogs.

'Kill him,' shouted a second zombie.

Arwel changed his mind; they were very threatening.

'Hit first, think second,' said the leader, shoving his second-in-command. 'You lost us the game through indiscipline.'

Number Two stepped back and hung his head.

'We won't kill you, Arwel,' said the leader, 'not yet, anyway. But if you tell anyone what you have seen here tonight . . . '

The other zombies began to chuckle: their voices sounded like branches snapping out of the trees.

'Our only pleasure is killing people, Arwel,' the zombie leader continued. He laughed mirthlessly.

Arwel nodded, although he couldn't quite see the joke. And how did the zombie know his name?

'Arwel,' the zombie repeated, extending his hand, 'we watched you play today; we understand your pain.' He pushed his hand out further. It was clear he wanted Arwel to shake it.

'How do you know my name?' stammered Arwel. 'How did you see the game?'

The zombie looked down at his hand, half-bone, half-flesh. 'We hide in the shadows; we creep through the drains; we knew the call was bad.'

Arwel looked at the hand, what was left of it. It was a blueish, grey colour, and the skin looked like batter mixture. Arwel put his hand out and slowly moved it towards the zombie's. He closed his eyes and gripped. The hand felt much stronger than he'd expected but cold and damp, like play dough. Arwel pulled his hand back, relieved to see that it was still pink. The zombie's hand stayed on his arm.

'I'm Delme, the fullback,' he said. 'You must come back to us.'

'What if I don't?' asked Arwel.

'You don't have a choice,' smiled Delme. All the zombies started to cackle. 'Come back tomorrow night,' said Delme. 'You are the only person who has ever visited us, the only one who can help us. You are the one we have been waiting for.'

The zombies began to slip quietly back into the forest. In no time they had disappeared. The silvery light that had lit them was gone. Now there was just silence.

Arwel stood up. Slowly, calmly, he walked out of the trees. He didn't feel scared at all.

Chapter 7

The next day in school was weird. Everybody laughed at Arwel for his mistake on the rugby pitch, but he didn't care. All he could think about were the rugby zombies. He didn't tell Glen and Martin because he had promised not to and he wasn't sure what the zombies would do to them. He thought that there was a good chance they'd kill them, or at least turn them into zombies.

Instead of hanging out with Glen and Martin as he normally would – they were giving him a wide berth, anyway, sensing that he needed time on his own – Arwel went to the library at lunchtime. He'd never visited the library before. He thought he had, but when he walked in he realised he didn't actually know what was in there. The teachers were always on at them to go up the library to use the computers or read. But nobody thought they were serious; at least Arwel didn't. To his surprise, the library wasn't such a bad place. For a start it smelt of curry because it was next to the canteen kitchen. The only good food the canteen made, in Arwel's opinion, was curry and chips, and here he could smell them both. The library was warm too; outside it was cold and windy and the weak November sun seemed incapable of warming anything. There must have been something wrong with the library radiators: they were like toast.

There were a few racks of huge books, encyclo-paedias and dictionaries, for brain-box geniuses in the sixth form. There were some desks where smaller, geeky kids sat reading books about geeky stuff (computers mostly, as far as he could see). And there were a couple of computers for people to do research for projects. Nobody was using them. Next to the computers lay a file called the 'Computer Book'. He followed the instructions and signed his name in. He wrote: 'Arwel Williams – 12.30 – searching for "zombies".'

Then he went on the computer. He couldn't find much because most of the websites he tried to access were filtered; those that weren't came up with conflicting information. Some said zombies were living people (but half-dead). Others that they were dead people (but half-living). Others said that they were controlled by voodoo magic from an island in the Caribbean. Or Africa. Or South America. Others said that zombies just existed in horror films. Arwel had already proved that one wrong. He knew that zombies existed in the woods above town. But he didn't know why.

He flicked through the pages on the computer screen as fast as he could, reading quickly. He didn't notice someone coming up behind him. A voice interrupted his thoughts. 'Hiding up here?' asked Beth, smiling.

Arwel, who was thinking about zombies, screamed out loud. The geeky kids giggled at him. He didn't like that.

Beth looked shocked and took a step back as Arwel turned around. 'Sorry, Arwel. What's the matter?'

'I'm just highly strung,' he replied.

'Is it the game? I saw what happened. It wasn't your fault,' she said again.

Arwel smiled and said he was definitely OK. He liked Beth. He'd never really spoken to her before. He supposed that was because he'd never been to the library at lunchtime. He always hung around with Glen and Martin. On the touchline the previous day she'd looked freezing cold. Now she looked warmer, in her red Aberscary Comprehensive School fleece. She also looked older. Like she was in control.

'I'm in charge,' she said.

'What?' said Arwel.

' . . . of the library, every Friday lunchtime. I'm the library monitor. I make sure nobody nicks stuff and I check that the computer book is filled in properly. You'll have to change this,' she said, pointing to Arwel's entry. 'Put "project work" or something like that. You're not allowed to look for just anything you like. And certainly not zombies.'

Arwel looked at Beth. 'Why not?' he asked.

'Because the teachers won't like it,' she muttered, crossing out Arwel's entry in the book and writing "project work" carefully over the word "zombies".

Beth looked at the computer screen and started to read.

Arwel quickly flipped the page he'd been studying.

'Looks interesting,' she said.

'It's homework. For art,' muttered Arwel, unconvincingly.

'Actually I love zombies,' Beth enthused.

Arwel didn't know quite what to say. Part of him wanted to say something like, 'You wouldn't love them so much if you knew the ones I just met. For a start they smell horrible.' Part of him wanted to be cool and say, 'Oh yeah. Me too. Zombies are just great!' And part of him wanted to tell Beth to get lost and keep her nose out because he didn't really want to have anything to do with someone called a library monitor. But most of him remembered his promise to the zombies: he'd promised not to tell anyone anything. So he said nothing. He just sat there in front of the screen.

In the end Beth spoke. 'It's zombie movies I love. I've got loads of DVDs. Do you want to watch one with me?'

The conversation, Arwel felt, was going off course. Not that it seemed to have much of a direction anyway. Beth was asking him to watch a DVD. No girl from school had asked him to watch DVDs before, and, despite Beth being a library monitor, he really liked her. This was good. But it was also bad, because she would definitely want to know more about his interest in zombies.

'Come to my place after school,' she said.

Arwel looked around the room. He could barely speak. 'Fine,' he finally managed to say.

*

That afternoon in geography everybody kept going on about the 'Arwel move'. Whenever anybody did anything wrong they said they were 'doing an Arwel', but Arwel hardly noticed. His mind was racing: Beth had asked him to watch zombie films. She was a girl. She had pretty green eyes and trendy hair. Loads of the boys in his year fancied her. What possible reason could she have for bothering with him?

And then the zombies marched back into his mind. He'd promised that he'd go back to the woods that evening.

After school Arwel tried to avoid Glen and Martin, but they spotted him by the gate and trotted over. Glen punched Arwel on the arm and told him not to worry about the game. Martin told him that they were going to build another zombie trap in the woods that night.

'Please don't do that,' said Arwel uneasily.

Martin just laughed and said that Arwel had lost his nerve because of the game. He reckoned it would take a few days before he got back to normal; in the meantime, he and Glen were going to use the wheelie bins to make a better zombie trap.

As they walked, Arwel could see the turning for Beth's street getting closer; he hoped Beth wasn't around because he didn't really want Martin and Glen knowing that he was going to her house.

'I don't think zombie traps are a good idea,' he said, seriously.

'Why not?' asked Martin.

'Because you might just catch one,' said Arwel.

'Ah,' laughed Martin, 'we've taken precautions. Glen, show him.'

From his bag, Glen produced two pencils held together crosswise with an elastic band, and a clove of garlic which he'd stolen from the cookery labs (Arwel had no idea why the food-tech teachers insisted that their kitchens were referred to as laboratories).

Arwel stopped walking; he'd reached Beth's street. The others stopped too. Arwel tried to think of something to say, but he didn't need to. Beth crossed the road behind them, shouting at Arwel to join her. Martin and Glen watched, shocked for a moment, then, whistling and laughing, they headed off to make their zombie traps.

Chapter 8

Beth's house was nice. It was clean, tidy, comfortable and normal. She lived with her mum, who was tall and had red hair. There were no rugby balls, drum kits or laptops.

Whilst they watched *Return from Zombie Island*, which was quite scary, Beth kept offering Arwel biscuits, and telling him what was going to happen next. Arwel watched the film quietly. He found it frightening, not because it was really freaky – it just reminded him of the real zombies.

When Beth's mum came into the TV room with more biscuits, she said, 'I'm sure Arwel has got better things to do than watch rubbish like this! Do you like horror films, Arwel?'

Beth answered for him. 'He loves them,' she said.

'Actually,' said Arwel. 'I dunno. They're OK. I prefer rugby, though.'

'Well, you're Mr Rugby's boy, aren't you? You're bound to,' laughed Beth's mum. She patted Arwel's shoulder; she felt that he might be an ally in the fight against her daughter's obsession with horror films.

'You have to be careful with dark forces,' Arwel went on. Beth's mum's face dropped – Arwel wasn't backing her up at all. 'In case you unleash powers beyond your control,' explained Arwel, earnestly.

Beth's mum tried to smile, but Arwel could tell this wasn't the answer she wanted.

Beth beamed. 'Exactly, Mum. That's why they're interesting.'

After the film Arwel went home and packed a bag. In it, he put a torch and his coat.

*

Later, when everybody was asleep, he crept downstairs, picked up his bag and let himself out of the front door. He hurried along the empty streets, wriggling into his coat. It was late. It was raining, a misty drizzle that shone in the streetlights. The town was silent; there were no people around, no cars. As he walked Arwel looked around him, scanning the side alleys and dark doorways, wondering if there were zombies hiding in the shadows, watching him. In the distance he could hear the scream of police cars; other than that all he could hear was the squelching of his trainers in the puddles.

Slowly, Arwel got closer to his goal, walking uphill through the empty, slimy streets then past the houses towards the forest. Once in the pine trees, he turned on his torch. He passed the wheelie bins which had been laid on their sides, nets and stakes positioned in front of them. Arwel looked inside. Beefburgers! Arwel shook his head. Glen and Martin. What a pair of idiots, he thought: firstly for trying catch zombies with beefburgers and secondly for messing with things they didn't understand. He hurried on, deep into the woods, until he found the spot where he had last encountered the zombies.

He switched off his torch and waited under the damp, dripping, black trees. It was cold, dark, lonely. He was scared; he wanted to go home, but part of him wanted to see the zombies once more, even though he couldn't be sure whether they were friendly or not. Arwel sniffed the air; he could smell that same musty scent – chip fat and mushrooms.

Before long the trees started to rattle. Arwel caught his breath. This was it. The zombies were coming; their strange silver, icy light began to make the night shine.

'You came back,' said Delme, emerging into the clearing.

'I promised,' said Arwel. 'You said you needed help.'

'You're a brave boy,' said Delme, 'or stupid. A lot of kids would be tucked up in bed. Aren't you scared?'

Arwel nodded. 'What do you want?' he asked.

The other zombies began crawling out of the trees. 'We don't want to be zombies any more,' said Delme.

Arwel looked at the decaying creatures: it wasn't surprising; they weren't very nice. 'Have you been cursed?' he whispered.

'Kind of. We played a game and we lost. This is the price of losing.'

'What happened?' asked Arwel.

'Rugby,' said Delme.

Arwel nodded; he understood; rugby could be great, but it could be bad too. He thought about his last game. If only he'd told them to change the call. He'd known it was the wrong call all along.

'We all have one thing in common,' explained Delme. 'Look at our shirts. We all played for Wales . . . once. Many years ago we were the best. We were the top: wingers, fullbacks, number eights, you name it, best of our generation. But we all played just once. And then never again. Like you.'

'I could make a comeback,' said Arwel.

Delme gave Arwel a sideways look. 'We goofed. I was fullback: I dropped the ball; I stopped concentrating for just one second – they scored a try and won the game.' Before hanging his head in shame Delme surveyed the other zombies: 'Tell him, boys, tell him your stories.'

The hooker, Number Two, stepped forward. 'I was undisciplined; I punched a guy; I gave away a crucial penalty; we lost,' he said.

The Number Eight stepped up next. 'I wasn't thinking straight; I missed a tackle; they scored under the posts; I never forgave myself.'

And another, one of the three-quarters this time: 'I missed touch; I didn't mean to, but just for a moment I stopped thinking; before I could do anything, they were in, and I was out.'

Suddenly the zombies were clamouring for attention, all shouting at once.

'I was done for obstruction.'

'I never looked outside. I never passed. If I'd passed we'd have won, but I wanted the glory for myself.'

And so it went on – fourteen sad stories from men who had let the team down. Suddenly Arwel knew why he was there. Or he felt he did. 'I misheard a move,' he said. 'I ran the wrong way; they scored; we lost.'

'You know what it's like then.' Delme put a decaying hand on Arwel's shoulder.

Arwel looked at it dubiously. 'I still don't get why you need me.'

'Well,' said Delme, 'it's simple. We didn't know this when we were alive. But there's a curse here in Wales, a zombie curse. When you play for Wales it's a great honour. You try as hard as you can. Win or lose it's the same. It's good to win. But you can't win all the games; sometimes the other side beats you. You can lose with pride, but if you feel wrong about it, it haunts you. If you think it's your fault, you are eaten up by it. You can't rest. The only way out of it is to win.'

'What are you saying?' asked Arwel, confused.

'We're zombies because we can't forgive ourselves,' said Delme. 'We'll only be released if we can put it right. And the only way to do that is to play another international – and win. Then we can be free.'

'But you're dead. How can you be free?' asked Arwel.

The zombies' laughter sounded like dry trees hitting the ground.

'Betwixt and between,' said Delme, 'not dead, not alive: we're in the dark.'

'What I mean is,' explained Arwel, 'you're too . . . decomposed to play an international. You're too old.'

'We can still play,' insisted Delme. 'Zombies are strong and fast; we have incredible powers; there's just one problem.'

'What?' asked Arwel, looking around. He could see a lot more than one problem.

'There are only fourteen of us; we need fifteen for a team.'

Arwel started to laugh: he couldn't stop himself. He laughed so much his sides hurt. 'You think that only having fourteen players is holding you back?' he spluttered. 'You're mad: you can't possibly play rugby; you'd decompose in sunlight; bits of you would drop off if anybody tackled you and . . . well, nobody in their right mind would play a game against you. And in any case, I'm thirteen and I've just been dropped from the school team – I can't play an international. Nobody would take us seriously.'

Delme looked on sadly. 'You take us seriously,' he said. 'You're going to be our fifteenth player – our outside half. If you play with us, you'll take on our powers on the pitch – you'll be as strong as any man.'

Arwel stopped laughing; he blinked as Delme paced up and down in frustration.

'You will play for us,' insisted the zombie captain. 'We will make a great team; we will win an international. Watch!' He turned to the zombies. 'OK, boys, let's show him what we can do.'

Arwel looked on as the zombies formed up. The pack was impressive; they practised by crunching down trees. The backs threw a rock around at bullet speed. Delme jogged over to Arwel. 'Well?' he said. 'You need a win too.'

Arwel spoke without thinking. 'I can't play rugby; I'm no good.'

'I thought you'd say that,' smiled Delme. 'Don't you see, Arwel, if you think like that you'll end up just like us. You have to play for us.'

Arwel shook his head, miserably. 'I can't do it; I'm not good enough; I'm not even good enough to get a photo onto my own mantelpiece,' he sniffed.

Delme frowned and tapped Arwel's shoulder. 'Look,' he said.

Delme nodded and a couple of zombies trotted off into the gloom. Moments later they returned, pushing two captives, both boys. Arwel recognised them instantly. They were Glen and Martin. They looked petrified.

'We found them building zombie traps,' laughed Delme. 'Not a very sensible thing to do.'

'Arwel, you gotta help us,' yelled Glen. 'They smell terrible.'

'The garlic didn't work,' muttered Martin.

'We're rugby zombies – we eat garlic for breakfast,' grinned Delme. 'Now, Arwel, we want you to play for us. If you do that we'll let these two idiotic friends of yours go. If you don't, we'll eat them!'

Arwel didn't have to think. He couldn't let the zombies eat his mates, even though they'd been incredibly stupid. He nodded. 'OK. But you're going to have to come out of these woods. You can't play rugby in a forest; you're going to have to trust me.'

'We do,' said Delme. 'Though we can't trust these two.'

The zombies had untied Glen and Martin; they stood shivering in the silvery light.

'Ah,' said Arwel, 'Glen and Martin. You might need them too. If we're going to play an international we're going to need all the friends we can get.'

'Trust us,' wailed Glen. 'We're nice guys.'

'We'll see,' said Delme, pushing Glen and Martin towards Arwel, the three of them huddling together. Arwel suddenly looked confident, almost as if he he'd been striking deals with zombies all his life. Martin looked shell-shocked whilst Glen muttered under his breath, apologising for all the bad things he had ever done.

'You play for the Zombies, now,' said Delme as he backed off into the forest. With that, the silver light began to fade and so did the rest of his team; they slid back into the woods, and soon, like puffs of smoke, they were gone.

Martin and Glen looked wide-eyed at Arwel: they had never seen, heard, felt or smelt anything quite like it. 'Mun!' said Martin. 'You were awesome.'

Arwel shook his head. 'We were awful,' he groaned. 'Come on, it's late. Your parents will be wondering where you are.'

*

Much later Arwel crawled back into bed. The police had been out looking for Martin and Glen; their parents had gone ballistic. Arwel had to sneak home in the shadows like a zombie himself. He pushed his key into the lock on the front door and turned it slowly; it flicked over with a tiny click, muffled by the raindrops. He kicked his shoes off and tiptoed into the house and up to his room. Finally he climbed into his own bed, pulled the sheets around him and plonked his pillow over his head. He was safe.

But he couldn't sleep. He lay awake, listening to the rain on his window, wondering how to arrange a game for a bunch of zombies.

Chapter 9

The next day in school Arwel went back to the library at dinner time to go online. He was tired and rubbed his eyes as he stared at the computer screen. Beth was already there. She came and slid onto the chair next to his. 'Do you want to watch *Realm of the Living Dead* after school?'

Arwel shuddered.

'Are you OK?' asked Beth.

Beth looked straight into Arwel's eyes: she could see he looked tired and worried. Her gaze made Arwel feel weird, as if she was examining his thoughts. What was the point of trying to hide anything? He was scared. He'd met zombies; they'd threatened to eat his friends and they wanted him to play outside half and arrange an international rugby match.

'Are the boys still laughing at you because of the game?' asked Beth.

'No,' said Arwel. 'I can't talk here. It's much more serious than that.'

Beth's eyes widened; she looked almost pleased. She liked the idea that Arwel wanted to tell her something. That made her special. Arwel glanced through the window; in the distance, bouncing a basketball under a hoop, stood two boys; they were equally worried.

'Look,' Arwel announced suddenly, standing up. 'I've got to go – see you after school.'

He hurried off, leaving Beth tapping on the screen, no doubt reading about zombies. He sneaked out through the fire door near the library and onto the playing fields. He ran towards the two boys on the basketball court.

When Arwel arrived, Glen and Martin were quiet, just bouncing the ball between them. The sound of the ball beating on the ground filled the silence; somehow it made things seem more normal. None of them could quite believe what they had seen. The zombies had changed their lives forever. They felt strange, as if the world they were in had changed and wasn't real any more, or as if they'd seen something that changed what the world really meant. Whichever it was, they knew something big had happened and it had altered everything. It made school seem small; it made the Spar seem a stupid place to hang out; it made the wheelie bins pointless; it made almost everything unimportant.

Martin flicked the basketball at Glen. 'It makes you think, doesn't it?'

Glen lined up a shot. 'If it makes you think, Martin, it's big.' The ball flopped through the hoop. He glared and nodded towards Arwel standing on the side of the court. 'Well, I'm glad I'm not in his shoes,' he said. 'At least I haven't got to play rugby with a bunch of zombies.'

'That's what I mean,' explained Martin. 'If Arwel goofs again – we're gonna be dead. Quite literally.'

'Actually,' said Glen, 'he's not a bad player. He just makes the odd tactical mistake.' An idea was forming in his head: 'We need an Arwel training programme.'

'Stop messing about, you two,' called Arwel. 'Stop talking about me like I'm not here.'

Martin caught the ball and sat on it. He looked out across the valley; little rows of terraced houses crawled up the hillsides like caterpillars. He could see his own house at the top of the hillside and next to it a forest full of snoozing zombies.

'You're right,' he agreed. 'Assuming these zombies are real and serious, and they do seem to be both of those things, Arwel's going to have to improve. You think he has potential? As a player? To be a match winner?'

Glen replied slowly, thoughtfully, 'I'm just saying he's not as bad as everybody reckons. If he had more confidence he could actually be quite good.'

'How good?' shouted Arwel, red with frustration. 'How good could I be?' He felt weird. He could be good; he knew he could.

'You could be great,' Glen conceded, 'but then again . . .'

'OK,' said Martin. 'I know what to do. You deal with the physical side of things. I'll concentrate on his mind. I need to develop his hidden depths.'

'Hidden depths?' asked Glen, ignoring Arwel once again. 'What do you mean?'

'That's why you do the fighting and I do the thinking,' said Martin. 'They're hidden . . . and they're deep. You can't say what they are straight away. We're going to turn that boy into a winner – a force to be reckoned with. Either that, or we're dead.'

'Do I get a say in any of this?' Arwel had moved away from the sideline, determined to get a toehold in the conversation.

'No!' chorused Glen and Martin.

'OK,' said Arwel slowly. 'But Beth's in on it too.'

'You've got to be joking!' Martin looked incredulously at his friend.

'Take it or leave it,' said Arwel.

*

Later that day four figures – Glen, Martin, Arwel and Beth – walked out of the school gates together. They said nothing. Things had changed.

Chapter 10

Arwel and Beth ate biscuits in the living room and Beth's mum brought them cups of tea. *Realm of the Living Dead* was on the screen, but Arwel wasn't watching – his eyes flicked nervously around the room. There were plenty of pictures of Beth on *her* mantelpiece. She stopped the film. 'What's the matter?' she asked. 'You're not watching.'

'I am,' said Arwel defensively.

'Tell me what's just happened then.'

'When?'

'Just then,' said Beth.

Arwel thought but he couldn't remember anything. 'Turn it back on. It'll come back to me.'

Beth tutted and went to restart the DVD. Arwel stopped her. 'Do you believe in horror?' he asked, deliberately.

Beth paused. 'Well – yes, I suppose so – it's scary, so the horror part of it is real,' she said, looking slightly confused.

'Not in films. In the real world,' persisted Arwel. 'Do you think there's such a thing as horror?'

Beth looked hard at Arwel; he could see huge question marks in her eyes. 'I don't know what you mean.'

'Do zombies exist?' he asked.

Beth restarted the film. 'Well, some people think so,' she said. 'In some of the Caribbean islands whole villages do. And loads of places in central Africa. People have written books about it.'

'But if I said there was a bunch of zombies,' Arwel spoke slowly, carefully, 'living in the forest behind Martin's house, you wouldn't think I was a nutter?'

Beth paused the film. 'I probably would,' she laughed. 'What kind of zombies?'

'Welsh ones,' said Arwel, '. . . rugby zombies.'

Beth rolled her eyes and sighed. 'You're nuts. You're just obsessing about that rugby game. It wasn't your fault; I've told you,' she said, starting the film again.

'I'm telling you, Beth, there is a bunch of rugby-playing zombies in that forest, and they want me to play for them. I can show you. Martin and Glen have seen them.' Arwel reached for the remote and switched off the TV. 'I need your help,' he said.

He wasn't sure whether Beth believed him. It didn't help that his zombies were Welsh and that they were wearing rugby kit. He'd found nothing on the internet about zombie rugby players.

When Arwel finished talking, Beth sat and thought for a minute. She nibbled at her biscuit. Then, without a word, she walked out, leaving Arwel on his own. Arwel inspected the neat little room. Beth's mantelpiece was covered in pictures, mostly of her: with the netball team; with the Brownies from when she was small; with her friends. He picked up a school photo and looked at her staring out at him. Even in the picture her eyes seemed to shine.

Suddenly the door kicked open and Beth struggled in, carrying two huge files. 'Give us a hand,' she said as she tried to balance the door with her foot.

Arwel took the files from her and put them down on the floor. He sat on the carpet and picked up the pink one. It had 'Alien Abductions' written on the outside in neat blue biro. Inside, Beth had kept newspaper cuttings and printouts from the internet. There was an article from the local paper about a man from Ponty who claimed to have seen extraterrestrials outside his uncle's pub.

Beth lay on the carpet, carefully leafing through the files, looking for anything she could find about Welsh zombies. She fired questions at Arwel: 'What kind of age were they? Where do they want to play? Who do they want to play? Could you disguise them in any way? Do they have any special powers?'

Arwel looked at her in amazement; who would have thought that a netball-playing library monitor would know so much about the supernatural? He tried to answer all of Beth's questions as fully as he could. He'd already figured out that the zombies would have to wear new kit: they could bandage up the bits that were falling off, maybe use scrum caps to hold their ears on; in fact, he reckoned that with brand-new kit nobody would be able to tell that they were really zombies.

'From the touchline, you can't see much anyway,' said Beth.

Arwel felt so relieved that she appeared to be taking it seriously. Either that or she thought he was so mad she just had to humour him.

Beth's mum popped her head into the TV room. 'Everything all right? I was just getting worried: you're very quiet.'

'We're doing homework,' said Beth, sitting on the floor, engrossed in her file.

Arwel looked up from the piece of paper he was reading, and smiled.

'Biscuits?' asked Beth's mum.

'Yes, please,' said Beth and her mum hurried off.

'Night fixtures only,' Arwel pointed out. 'Zombies don't like sunlight.'

'Moonlight would be best,' agreed Beth.

Arwel smiled.

Chapter 11

When Arwel finally got home he wasn't hungry. Tania and Steve were sitting at the kitchen table and Dad was doing Buddhist drumming upstairs. They could hear him chanting.

'There,' said Arwel's mum, handing out bowls of stew.

Dad came bounding in, attracted by the smell. 'This is nice,' he said, breezing into the room, 'a family meal.'

'We don't eat together enough,' said Mum.

'Well,' said Tania, 'just so long as you know we're going out later.'

Arwel's mum served the stew. Arwel saw his chance. 'Err, Dad,' he said.

'Err, what?' his dad replied, irritatingly.

'It's about rugby,' said Arwel. 'I've had an idea.'

His dad looked glum.

'Don't worry, Arwel,' said Steve. 'You'll get another break.'

Arwel persisted: 'What if I said that I'd formed a new team and that we're looking for a game?'

'Oh, Arwel,' sighed Mum, 'don't you think you should do something else for a while?'

'Yeah, like tiddlywinks,' laughed Tania.

'Arwel's a good player,' said Steve. 'He just didn't hear the call.'

'Not as good as you though,' said Tania.

Steve had to agree that this was true; Arwel was not as good as him; in fact very few people were.

'What about this team of mine?' asked Arwel.

'It's a secret team, is it? Arwel's Amateurs?' sneered Tania.

'We'd give you a game,' said Dad. 'The Thirds are always looking for worthy opponents.'

'No,' said Arwel, 'we're good; we want to play the Firsts – in a "friendly".'

'A "friendly",' repeated Dad, chewing a piece of lamb. A wistful look crossed his face. 'We haven't had a "friendly" for years.'

'No,' said Mum, 'and with good reason. Friendlies are terrible. I remember them; that's why they were banned, all that fighting . . .'

Arwel's dad recalled countless 'friendlies' at the club. The most brutal matches he ever played in. 'Friendlies' were relics of a bygone age, before people got paid for playing. In those days rugby was tribal.

'You haven't even got a team,' interrupted Tania.

'I have,' insisted Arwel. 'I've got everyone: Martin and Glen have met the boys; we just want a chance.'

'What are you called?' asked Tania.

Arwel hadn't thought of this. He paused. 'The Zombies,' he said.

Dad popped a potato into his mouth. 'The

Zombies,' he repeated, sucking thoughtfully. 'I feel good karma about this. If Arwel and his mates want to play a friendly, I'll see what I can do. Steve, are you in? It'll have to be midweek – an evening kick-off.'

Steve smiled: of course he'd play. He liked Arwel, the game would be a waste of time, but he could see it might help Arwel's confidence as a player, and the boy deserved a second chance.

'Hmm. I don't see how a spiritually enlightened peace lover can possibly be interested in rugby friendlies,' said Mum.

*

Later that night Arwel sent a message to Glen, Martin and Beth: 'Game on!'

Chapter 12

'We've got to improve your mental approach,' said Martin halfway across the rec.

'I don't see how getting Glen to sit on me is helping,' grunted Arwel from underneath his friend.

Glen stood up and allowed Arwel to clamber off the ground.

'I've programmed Glen to attack at will. When you least expect it he will pounce,' said Martin. 'You've got to be ready at all times to expect the unexpected and to out-think his superior skills and physical power.'

Glen dropped his shoulder and charged into Arwel, who was brushing grass off his trousers, driving Arwel back across the grass until he fell over again.

Martin trotted over to him, lying flat on the turf. 'You've got to play like you know what you're doing,' he said. 'At the moment you're a lightweight makeweight.'

Glen had mysteriously acquired a plank from a skip. Now he used it to charge at Arwel, forcing him to jink and sidestep to avoid the blows.

'Brilliant!' yelled Martin. 'Now you're thinking, Arwel.'

'No, I'm not,' screeched Arwel, ducking to avoid a sideswipe from the plank.

'Physical violence without brainpower isn't going to achieve anything, Glen,' shouted Martin.

Glen attacked with his plank for ten more minutes before he finally ran out of energy. At last, he put the piece of wood down; it was an old skirting board. 'Nice one,' he panted.

When Arwel laughed, Glen grabbed him in a headlock, wrestled him to the floor and sat on his chest again.

'Rooky error,' said Martin, pulling Glen off. 'He's a killing machine; don't forget that.'

Arwel scrambled to his feet. 'OK, I get the picture.'

*

The next few days were bad for Arwel. It didn't matter where he was: in lessons, in the canteen, walking home, even up in the forest. Glen's physical attacks were relentless.

And then came the breakthrough. They were all queuing up for school dinner: Arwel was complaining to Martin about the training programme, but Beth was taking Martin's side: Arwel just had to become brilliant at slipping tackles and this was the only way to improve. Arwel had his tray in his hands and the dinner lady had just popped a load of curry and chips on his plate. He turned and was walking to his table when he spotted Glen emerging from behind a crowd of year 7s like a shark speeding through the shallows.

Glen made a dive, but Arwel was too quick and leapt on his friend, sending him sprawling to the floor. The cooks screamed and curry went everywhere, as the teachers tried to pull the two boys apart. The year 7s watched, open-mouthed, whilst Martin and Beth punched the air and shouted: 'Yessss.'

'That is what I call a result,' said Martin. 'He's thinking in the moment; he's not worried about the consequences of his actions.'

'Not bad,' Glen conceded, scrambling to his feet. 'I'd have got him in the end though.'

'Ah, but you didn't,' said Martin.

Beth was really pleased. 'Fantastic!' she shouted as she pulled Arwel back up onto his feet. 'That deserves a reward. All of you, come back to my house after school.'

Arwel smiled; he felt good. He didn't know quite why, because he'd lost his curry and chips, but he didn't suppose that mattered much. He and Glen got three weeks' worth of detention from Miss Tavernspite and letters home for fighting which said that they would be excluded if it happened again.

*

After school the three boys made their way to Beth's house. She told them to wait in the TV room while she went to fetch their reward. Martin picked up one of the photos from the mantelpiece.

'Careful,' warned Arwel, taking it from him and putting it back.

The door opened and Beth struggled in with two huge bin bags. 'Come on, give us a hand,' she grunted.

They lugged the bags in front of the TV and tipped the contents on the floor. Beth gazed with pride and started holding things up. 'Oxfam shop: rugby jersey, 50p; socks, 10p; look – boots, everything. I've even found some skull caps for the forwards.'

The boys gasped – it was kit, a complete team's kit. Old, and the jerseys were all different colours, but it was much better than the decomposing tatters the Zombies normally wore.

'If they're going to play, they'll have to look human,' said Beth.

Her mum popped her head around the door. 'Biscuits anybody?'

'No thanks,' they all chorused, so she smiled and went away again.

'Wow,' said Martin, 'all we need now is a game. We win that, we win the next and the next and then . . .'

'OK,' said Arwel, 'so can you stop attacking me with sticks?'

Martin and Beth exchanged glances then Beth said firmly, 'No, I'm afraid not. You have to be ready for anything!'

As if to underline her point, Glen jumped on Arwel

at once and started wrestling him. Arwel tried to speak as he defended himself. 'I'll go and see Delme,' he panted, 'fix up a date. The Zombies versus Aberscary – the first "friendly" for years – it'll be a sell-out!'

*

As Delme paced up and down on the pine needles, Arwel saw that his tattered number 15 jersey actually did have mushrooms growing out of the shoulders.

'A friendly,' muttered Delme, rubbing his chin.

'It's not an international – it's only Aberscary – but we have to win some games before we can play an international, that's obvious,' said Arwel.

'A game,' shouted Delme, turning to Arwel, 'a real game!'

There was a strange look on his face. Arwel supposed it was the nearest thing a zombie could get to a smile. He looked again. Yes, definitely a smile.

Delme grabbed Arwel's shoulders. 'Brilliant, boy, I knew you could do it; this is the best news I've had for . . . fifty years.' Suddenly Delme's laughter turned to tears.

'Don't cry,' whispered Arwel. 'Why are you crying?'

'It's nothing,' sniffed Delme, adjusting his right eye. 'I'm just . . . well, very emotional. You've seen the players crying when they play the anthems? I used to do that all the time. I think I'm going to have to sit down.'

He sat, resting his back against a pine tree until he composed himself again. 'Where? When? How?' he asked.

'We've got kit, we've got a pitch and a team to play against,' said Arwel. 'You tell the zombies to get ready. Leave the rest to me.'

'You'll play outside half?' asked Delme.

'Of course,' said Arwel. 'I've been practising.'

Delme stood up, clearly feeling better. 'Sorry about that, boy; I just . . . I can't believe it. I can't wait to tell the boys. They'll want to know the date though.'

Arwel said the first thing that came into his head: 22 November. He had no idea what day of the week it was even but it made him sound like he'd planned everything properly. And for some reason the date was lodged in his memory.

'Great! Next week!' said Delme, hurrying off. 'Good work, boy. No time like the present, eh? Can't wait to tell the others.' With that, Delme ran off into the darkness, laughing and shouting as he went.

As Arwel left the forest he could hear strange noises coming from deep inside the darkness. It sounded like trees falling over. He guessed it was the sound of zombies doing high fives.

*

Next day at school it was big news that Arwel had arranged a 'friendly'. Even the teachers wanted to know just who was in his mystery team.

Everybody thought it was a cool idea. Except for Gilligan, who wasn't impressed. Gilligan was hard. Gilligan was a bully. Gilligan liked Beth.

On his way home, Arwel was trying to hide from Glen, who was chasing him with a baseball bat, when he ran straight into his old enemy outside the Spar.

'Well, if it isn't Mr Rugby Junior,' said Gilligan.

'Hiya, Gilligan,' stammered Arwel, wishing he hadn't done such a good job of losing Glen.

Gilligan's small blue eyes glittered with malice. 'You really think you're something, don't you? But after that fiasco against Ponty, in your one and only appearance for the team, nobody wants you. To get any kind of game you have to arrange your own! I tell you what: I'm going to make sure I play in this "friendly" of yours.' He pushed Arwel in the chest. When the smaller boy didn't respond, he pushed him again, harder. Arwel fell back against the rank of new wheelie bins.

At that moment, Glen came speeding round the corner with his improvised baseball bat, catching Gilligan off guard. Arwel scrambled to his feet and made his escape. When he reached the rec., closely followed by Glen, there was no sign of Gilligan. 'Nice one,' he panted.

'I don't think this training is working so well,' said Glen. 'How did you let Gilligan corner you like that?'

'I was running away from you,' said Arwel.

Glen laughed and rugby-tackled him.

Arwel felt that he was in some kind of weird nightmare. All day he was under threat of attack, and at night he discussed strategy and tactics with an un-dead rugby player called Delme. At home his dad could talk about nothing but the 'friendly' and how Arwel's team was going to get mashed. He seemed to have forgotten that his son was playing at outside half. Even Beth wasn't much help. She just kept reading terrifying facts about zombies from her files.

What would happen if they lost? Arwel had never won a game of rugby in his life. The original curse on the zombies had happened because they lost. If they lost again, they'd surely take it out on Arwel and his mates.

Or, at the very least, on Arwel.

Chapter 13

The night of 22 November was cold and dark. The little clubhouse in Aberscary was a hive of activity. There was a burger van parked near the pitch and steam hissed from its outsize tea urn. Beneath the orange glow of the bar, the regulars clutched their pints of beer. Cars arrived from all over the district, bringing in players and supporters. Old men who hadn't been seen at the ground in living memory came down with their sticks and dogs to see the first 'friendly' for years. The changing rooms clattered to the sound of shouts and studs. The club secretary (Arwel's dad), the treasurer (his friend Benbow) and the chairman (Wayne Hoof's dad) leant on a railing, looking at the floodlit pitch. Tania stood nearby, wrapped in a long blue coat. She had a face like thunder. It was her birthday. Why, she asked everybody, had Arwel chosen her birthday to play his 'friendly'? She thought it was a deliberate plan to spoil her special day.

'Beautiful, isn't it?' said Hoof, admiring the posts pointing up into the starry night sky.

Benbow looked around at the colourful scene: the lurid floodlit grass; the bright winter clothes; the glow of the clubhouse. He rubbed his beard; this usually meant he was thinking.

'No sign of these Zombies, whoever they are,' he said. 'Are they coming in a minibus?'

Arwel's dad wasn't sure. 'All I know is that they'll be here at the ground at seven-thirty,' he said.

Benbow stroked his beard even more. 'Are you sure your boy's not having us on?' he asked.

Arwel's dad shook his head and mopped his brow with the sleeve of his Aberscary jersey. 'He may be an idiot sometimes, but he's a good boy. If he says he's going to do something, he'll do it.'

Up in the woods it was chaos. Arwel, Martin, Beth and Glen were handing out equipment. Anyone with open wounds had to have them bandaged; all sorts of knee braces and arm protectors were needed. It took a long time but in the end everyone was dressed in their 'new' kit. The Zombies looked conspicuous to say the least: hooped, striped, and quartered, their second-hand jerseys were a kaleidoscope of different colours.

Beth took a step back to admire them. 'Wonderful,' she announced. 'In the old days players wore their club colours when they played for the Barbarians.'

Delme laughed. 'We're not the Barbarians – we're the Zombies.' He turned to Arwel, who was wearing his school kit. 'Skip, you got a few words for the boys? They're a bit rusty,' he said quietly. 'They need a bit of encouragement.'

Arwel looked at the team lined up in front of him. They expected him to say something. Martin and Glen looked pointedly at him.

'Go on,' whispered Beth, shoving him in the back.

'OK,' said Arwel, 'today we're playing my dad's team, Aberscary. I know it's not the international game you want. I know you need to play a real international. But we can't do it yet, not without earning it. We have to start small and get big. We have to make a name for ourselves.'

He could see the pitch shining in the floodlights about a mile away down the hillside.

'They're going to throw everything at us. They haven't played a "friendly" for years. Just remember this: you may think you made a mistake some time ago; you may believe that you can never put it right; but what you do next is always more important than what you did last. If you know what's right, you'll do it. And remember this. We're a team. We are the Zombies. There is nobody quite like us.' He paused for a moment to let his words sink in. 'Now, we've been waiting long enough: let's walk down there and win that game!'

Delme wiped a tear from his eye. 'All right,' he sniffed as they tramped down towards the ground.

'I'm a bit worried about the floodlights,' whispered Martin. 'Won't it dissolve them?'

'No,' said Beth, 'though sunlight would. Floodlights are fine.'

Back at the ground, Arwel's dad and his mates were pacing up the touchline. The Aberscary team were jogging up and down too.

'I hate to say this,' said Benbow, 'but I think your boy must have forgotten.'

'Maybe he's scared,' suggested Hoof.

The committee looked at Arwel's dad sideways – it took a great deal of work to put on a 'friendly'; a lot of players had given up their evenings for this.

'No,' he said. 'Arwel will be here any minute now, and his team, they're probably just . . . oh my goodness . . .' His voice trailed off as he looked across the pitch.

Slowly the Aberscary team stopped jogging.

Benbow and Hoof stopped pacing the touchline. The man on the burger van dropped his frankfurter. Tania and the spectators stared, open-mouthed.

Everybody fell silent, and watched as the Zombies came out of the night. A multi-coloured troupe of misfits, an army of strangers, all of them ugly (apart from Arwel). Really, really ugly; really, really, really ugly. It was the ugliest team Arwel's dad had ever seen.

'Your boy's been hanging around with some very funny types,' said Benbow.

'Well,' agreed Dad, 'they're definitely not Buddhists.'

'They don't look like rugby players either; they're a bit old,' said Hoof.

The Zombies emerged onto the field. Beth, Martin and Glen made their way to the touchline. As team manager, Martin was wearing shiny shoes and a jacket he'd been bought once to go to a funeral. The trainer, Glen, wore a brown tracksuit. Beth carried a bucket and sponge (she was team physio). Concealed inside the bucket she had a big roll of tape – which she'd use to attach any broken pieces of zombie.

The teams took up their positions. Arwel stood at fly half.

'Oh, Christmas,' groaned his dad. 'I can't watch this – Steve'll mash him.'

Arwel gave a thumbs-up to Glen on the touchline. He felt confident – Glen's rigorous training programme had paid off. He felt as if nobody was going to touch him.

In front of him was the opposition: Steve, Gilligan and a selection of his dad's mates from the club. All around the ground he could feel the eyes of an expectant crowd: kids from school, Beth's mum – he could see her red hair – even Mr Edwards, they'd all turned out to watch.

Behind him Arwel could hear Delme sniffing and snivelling, overcome by memories of countless games in the past.

Steve flipped the ball to Arwel who held it up for everyone to see. Then he kicked off. The ball hit the ground, bounced and smack! Arwel's boot connected with it sweetly. It soared like a missile high into the air. 'Game on,' whispered Arwel. This was it.

The first exchanges went badly for the Zombies. Some of them hadn't played for over fifty years. They weren't used to the feel or speed of the ball, and they'd forgotten lots of the basic skills . . . like catching. The pack wasn't together; they were strong as individuals, but weak as a group. At first Arwel was the only one who showed any confidence. He kicked for touch, he passed well, and he even managed to tackle Steve. Delme's prediction was right: on the pitch he was as strong as the adult players.

Arwel was not impressed when he heard his sister yelling: 'Go, Steve, flatten him!' nor when Gilligan thumped him. But it was heartening to hear Beth's full-throated shout: 'Gilligan, you big bully; pick on someone your own size.'

But despite Arwel's outstanding personal performance, the Zombies were soon losing. They were very rusty. They missed tackles, they lost the ball, they didn't know lots of the modern rules, and just before half-time they were down by twenty-five points to nil.

On the touchline Dad, Benbow, and Hoof were pleased that Aberscary were playing so well. But something was bothering Benbow. He tapped Arwel's father on the arm. 'That number 11, he's the spit of Gryff Griffiths, the Flying Wing. Remember him?'

Dad nodded; there was something familiar about several of the players in Arwel's team. They looked uncannily like players he remembered from years ago. He scratched his head. 'I know, I don't understand it,' he murmured. 'There's something very odd about that team.'

As the whistle blew for half-time, Martin, Glen and Beth ran out onto the pitch. The Zombies looked tired; they bent over to try and catch their breath.

Glen stepped forwards. 'That was terrible,' he shouted.

Delme hung his head, tears beginning to fill his eye.

'Call yourself Zombies?' continued Glen. 'You couldn't frighten a flea. They're killing you. The only one who's doing anything good is Arwel . . . and he's a human being. You're a disgrace to the underworld!'

The Zombies shuffled in their multicoloured socks.

'Come on, boys,' continued Glen. 'You're not thinking. Remember who you are, or were; you are great players; this is going to be the greatest team ever.'

The Zombies looked at one another, the message sinking in slowly. 'Yeah,' said Number Two. 'He's right,' and started to laugh. The others began to join in too.

'What on earth are they doing?' muttered Benbow from the touchline.

'I dunno,' said Arwel's dad. 'They're a funny bunch. Looks like they're laughing.'

'Your Arwel's playing well,' muttered Benbow. 'We should give him a run-out for the Thirds one day.'

'Aye,' agreed Arwel's dad, 'behind a retreating pack, in the face of a Welsh outside half and a psychotic winger who clearly wants to rip his head off, he's doing pretty well. But the rest of them haven't troubled us at all. We could put fifty points on them.'

The second half was a different story. The Zombies had begun to develop a feel for the ball and were starting to find their strength. The pack seemed to grow in confidence and size.

The fight back started behind the Zombies' twenty-two. The Aberscary forwards were pressing for a try when the ball went loose and the winger, Gryff, grabbed it. A little jink and a pass to Arwel who could only think of one thing. He'd have to kick for touch otherwise they'd score under the posts. But when he heard Gryff almost whisper the word 'outside' to him, he flicked the ball on for the Zombie winger, who'd looped around and run forward as fast as he could. Another jink from Gryff and they were in space. Gryff passed back to Arwel, who found himself skipping past Gilligan as easily as if he'd been Glen with his skirting board.

He could hear the winger's boots pounding the ground behind him and knew he'd soon be caught, so he chipped the ball to the right for Gryff to run on to just before he was crunched by one of the Aberscary wingers. With the fullback beaten and both wingers targeting Arwel, there was nobody who could get within a mile of Gryff. He collected the ball and tapped it down under the posts for the Zombies' first try.

The crowd fell silent. And then slowly they began to clap and cheer. They appreciated good rugby.

Gryff shouted to Arwel as they trotted back: 'Well done, boy; you made that try.'

Delme ran up and patted Gryff on the back. 'One hundred years old and still faster than an Olympic sprinter,' he laughed. 'Nice one, Gryff.'

From that moment on Arwel played . . . like a Zombie. He was brilliant. The Aberscary team was good, but their players didn't have anything to match the sheer skill of the Zombies. Slowly, they ground their opponents down. Gilligan missed a tackle and was taken off by the Aberscary trainer. The Aberscary front row began to wilt under the Zombies' spell. Another try came, then another, and another. Before long the Zombies were scoring at will, running like the wind, driving players out of the way like snowploughs crashing through snowmen. Thirty, forty, fifty points came up. More people arrived at the ground. The clubhouse emptied as the crowd crammed the touchline, trying to get a glimpse of the spectacle. It had turned into an exhibition of controlled, powerful, beautiful rugby. Passes spun flat for miles, kicks arrowed through the air and tackles crunched the opponents. Steve could barely believe his eyes: Arwel was controlling the game. At the end, the score was an unbelievable seventy-three points to twenty-five. Steve and Arwel shook hands as they walked off the field together.

'Who are they?' asked Steve. 'They're incredible.'

Arwel smiled. 'The Zombies,' he said.

He turned and looked across the pitch: the Zombies were exhausted: some of them lay on the grass as if they'd been shot; others bent over, trying to get their breath back. Beth ran between them, applying tape to some of the less solid players, trying to make sure that they didn't leave any fingers or feet on the field of play. Martin, meanwhile, was making a statement to the reporter from the local newspaper. Glen trotted around the pitch, urging the Zombies to join gyms and get fit.

Arwel's dad rushed over. 'Forget about the score, boy; that was the best "friendly" I've seen in years. Just who on earth are these guys?'

'Can't say, Dad, just a bunch of mates,' grinned Arwel, grabbing his father's arm and pulling him towards the clubhouse, safely away from the Zombies. 'They don't talk to anyone. They like to keep themselves to themselves.'

The Zombies were already melting away into the night, disappearing like ships into the mist. Seconds after the final whistle blew they were all gone.

'Incredible,' sighed Arwel's dad, as his battered and bruised Aberscary team limped back into the clubhouse. 'Listen, son,' he said, returning to the attack. 'You've got to tell me . . . your team, I know you don't want to give away any secrets, but . . . I've got to know who they are.'

'Just people,' bluffed Arwel.

'Not just people; they're some of the best rugby-playing talent I've ever seen. Where did you find them?'

'Around,' said Arwel, airily.

'They're an ugly bunch, but there's something about them,' persisted his dad. 'They're so familiar. One of them looks the spit of Gryff Griffiths, the Flying Wing: only capped once for Wales, but a legend even so. I thought he'd died twenty years ago. It was like watching a ghost from the past.'

He looked at Arwel, who avoided his gaze. He knew what his dad was thinking. He was currently a Buddhist, after all; he believed in reincarnation. He had an impossible thought in his head which Arwel was not going to discuss.

'Gotta go,' he said.

*

Later that night, Arwel, Martin, Beth and Glen went to the biggest zombie party ever held in the forest.

As well as all the old rugby songs, the Zombies had added a new chant all of their own. 'We're going to be free,' they sang.

As she watched Glen and Martin dancing around the trees with the Zombies, Beth whispered to Arwel, 'This is incredible; it's the most amazing day of my life.'

Arwel agreed, but he couldn't help feeling a little concerned. One by one the Zombies came up to him, asking, 'When's the international?' All he could do was smile and say 'soon' but the truth of the matter was he had absolutely no idea when or even if they would be able to play another game. And when they all linked arms and began chanting 'When? When? When?' he started to feel that familiar chill.

The Zombies had changed; Glen and Martin weren't dancing with them any more. They felt it too, that cold wind that gnawed into their ribs, the cold of the living dead.

Arwel, Beth, Glen and Martin drew closer together. They all felt the same, deeply, uncontrollably frightened. The Zombies were like wolves, one minute calm and friendly, the next a pack, thinking as one, instinctive, dangerous.

Beth whispered into Arwel's ear. 'This behaviour is typical – zombies can be light, but they can be very, very dark. This is bad, Arwel.'

'When! When! When!' screeched the Zombies, their faces black with a strange cold power.

'OK,' said Glen. 'I've got a new call. When I say it . . . do it.'

'Say it then,' hissed Arwel; the Zombies had almost surrounded them, their chanting now a hypnotic drone.

'They're in a trance,' whispered Beth. 'There's no telling what they might do. Zombies can turn suddenly like this. They're so close to the dark that it threatens to take them over. They will destroy anything, even their friends.'

'When! When! When!' the Zombies intoned, shuffling their feet and closing in. There was now only a tiny gap through which Arwel and the others could escape. Glen was so scared, he'd lost his voice; he couldn't make the call.

'Stop!' shouted Martin suddenly, an unexpected note of authority in his voice. 'I'm your manager; you have to listen to me! Now!'

The Zombies had almost completed their circle but they stopped in their tracks and looked up.

'Has Arwel ever let you down?' yelled Martin. 'He kept his promise, didn't he? If it wasn't for Arwel you wouldn't have had a game at all. You need to show him a bit of gratitude. And if you want an international, you're going to have to be a lot more cooperative.'

The Zombies hung their heads and mumbled apologetically, their kit looking grey and shapeless in the murky forest light. Delme broke free from his muddy companions. 'Sorry,' he said, his eye wobbling dangerously. 'We're a bit worked up. It's the excitement of winning after all these years. It's not that we aren't grateful for all you've done: we're behind Arwel all the way.' He turned to the Zombies. 'Aren't we, boys?'

The Zombies nodded, malevolently it seemed to Arwel.

Delme whispered: 'When they get excited, they're hard to control. Well, I suppose I am too.' He twitched slightly. 'If I were you, I'd get out of here. We can be a bit . . . unpredictable.'

Arwel had heard enough; it was time to go. He shoved Martin and Glen and pulled Beth's arm. 'Come on!' he called and the four of them dived past the Zombies and through the forest, their feet kicking up the pine needles as they charged headlong through the undergrowth.

The Zombies followed them, laughing like hyenas, cracking branches as they smashed through the trees. It was all part of the game as far as they were concerned. Delme ran behind the main pack, urging them to calm down and take it easy.

How Arwel made it back to Martin's he never knew. His prize team had turned into wild animals, charging at them from all angles. At last, puffing and wheezing, the four friends leaned against the relative safety of Martin's garden wall. Arwel looked back at the black forest. He imagined the Zombies within, cold, clacking like crabs, desperate for their next game.

'We have so got to get those boys an international,' muttered Martin, trying to get his breath back.

Arwel nodded. He felt cold, as if the Zombies were still watching him, following his every move.

'Whose team are they on?' whined Glen.

'They're just doing what comes naturally. They're not like us, but at least they're back onside,' said Beth.

'Great,' muttered Arwel.

*

The next day was surreal. The local newspaper had a front-page headline: 'WHO ARE THE ZOMBIES?' The paper was propped up on a cereal packet and Arwel's dad sat behind it, beaming.

'What a night!' he said as Arwel rummaged through the fridge, looking for cheese.

'You were just fantastic,' said Dad, 'a natural Number Ten.'

Arwel shrugged his shoulders modestly. 'It must have been the drumming, Dad,' he said.

His father looked thoughtful for a moment. He remembered the evening they had spent up in the meditation room and a smile crossed his face. 'Yeah,' he said. 'I suppose you're right,' realising that he too could take some credit for his son's performance.

In school everybody wanted to talk to Arwel about his new team. Martin and Glen were suddenly cooler than ice cream; even year 12s and 13s wanted to know them. All the girls were keen to talk to Beth. Everybody was wild to know who the Zombies were. But Arwel and the others knew they couldn't say anything. Somehow the cold they'd felt up in the forest had stayed with them.

Apart from the strange feeling of being under surveillance, only one bad thing happened. It took place on the way home from school, outside the Spar, when Gilligan grabbed Arwel. 'You may think you won the game, but I'm warning you. I'll find out what you're up to. You're just a nothing. Everyone needs to know that you're a fake! And that team of yours? I'm going to find out about them too.'

Arwel walked home alone, not sure quite how to feel. He had taken a team of un-dead hundred-year-old rugby players and won a real game. He had played brilliantly at outside half and he had captained the team. Nothing Gilligan could say or do could take that away from him. And if Gilligan decided to investigate the Zombies, well, he might get more than he bargained for.

A cloud passed in front of the sun, suddenly throwing Aberscary into shade. Arwel shivered. He thought about the Zombies, and that deathly cold deep in the black forest. He knew they wouldn't be satisfied with a small local win. Playing a 'friendly' against Aberscary was one thing, but it wasn't going to be enough. How was he going to get the team a real international match?

That, he knew, was going to be tricky.